D1404572

First edition for the United States and the Philippines published 1995 by
Barron's Educational Series, Inc.

First published 1993 by Piccadilly Press Ltd., London, England

All inquiries should be addressed to:
Barron's Educational Series, Inc.
250 Wireless Boulevard
Hauppauge, New York 11788

Library of Congress Catalog Card No.: 94-28923

International Standard Book No. 0-8120-9183-3 (paperback)
0-8120-6498-4 (hardcover)

Library of Congress Cataloging-in-Publication Data
Pizer, Abigail.
    Tippu / Abigail Pizer and David Day; illustrated by Abigail
Pizer.
        p.   cm.
    Summary: When hunters attack their herd, Tippu the elephant
and his sister get separated from the other elephants and begin a
long journey to a safe home.
    ISBN 0-8120-6498-4. — ISBN 0-8120-9183-3 (pbk.)
    1. Elephants—Juvenile fiction.   2. Animals—Juvenile fiction.
[1. Elephants—Fiction.   2. Animals—Fiction.   3. Game pre-
serves—Fiction.]   I. Day, David, 1947–   .   II. Title.
PZ10.3.P419Ti   1995
[E]—dc20   94-28923
                                                                    CIP
                                                                    AC

5678   9697   987654321

TIPPU

Abigail Pizer and David Day
Illustrated by Abigail Pizer

BARRON'S

Tippu and his sister live with their family on a wide grassy plain in Africa.

They eat lots of fresh grass and leaves.

One morning, trucks roar across the plain. The hunters have come in search of the elephants. They want elephant tusks for ivory jewelry. Guns are fired and the elephants flee in terror.

Tippu and his sister become lost. Then a friendly white stork arrives to help them.

"Come with me," says the stork. "I know a place that is safe for animals."

The young elephants follow the stork for many miles. Eventually, they come to a land that is scorched and black.

"Men have burned all the grass and the trees, and they have dammed up the river. Animals cannot live here now," explains the stork.

After leaving the scorched land, Tippu and his sister come across a sad little leopard.

"Hunters were here too," explains the leopard. "They wanted leopard skins to make into fur coats."

"Come with us," says Tippu. "We are going to a place that is safe for animals."

The animals find a little rhinoceros standing by a dry river. "The hunters were here," says the little rhinoceros. "They wanted rhinoceros horn to make into medicine."

"Come with us," says the leopard. "We are going to a place that is safe for animals."

The elephants, the leopard, and the little rhinoceros all follow the stork. Then trucks appear and a helicopter whirs overhead. The animals start to run.

Tippu hears shots. His legs feel weak, and he finds himself tumbling to the ground.

Tippu awakens in the truck with the other animals. The truck stops, and men gently lead the animals down to the grassy plain.

This place is safe for animals. Tippu begins to understand that not all men try to hurt animals. Some are good and gentle and helpful.

The little rhinoceros sees six other rhinoceroses wading in the water-hole. He is so happy to see them, he runs over and rubs horns.

A moment later, the leopard sees a family of leopards resting beneath a big tree. She runs over to play with the other baby leopard.

Tippu and his sister hear a loud trumpeting sound. Standing out on the plain is a herd of elephants. One of them is calling.

They have found their family. They are safe.